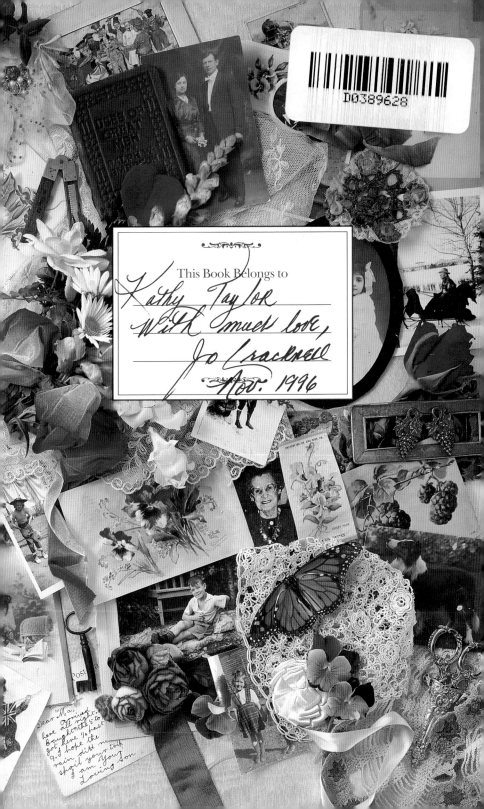

This Book Belongs to

Kathy Taylor
with much love,
Jo Cracknell
Nov. 1996

Recollections

by Judith Baker Montano

C&T PUBLISHING

To Dan,

with love, respect,

and trust

Copyright © 1993 Judith Baker Montano

Watercolors & illustrations © 1993 Kristine Smith

Edited by Harold Nadel
Book design by Jody Hubert Keisling & Judy Benjamin
Photography by Bill O'Connor
Cover conception & collages by Judith Baker Montano

Published by C & T Publishing
P. O. Box 1456
Lafayette, California 94549

Collages from the private collection of the author.
The author extends special thanks to Canada Pacific Railroad and
RagTime of Castle Rock, Colorado for the use of selected memorabilia.

ISBN 0-914881-59-0

Library of Congress Catalog Card Number: 92-44544

Library of Congress Cataloging-in-Publication Data
Montano, Judith.
    Recollections / by Judith Baker Montano.
        p.   cm.
    ISBN 0-914881-59-0
    I. Title.
    PR9199.3.M597R4   1993
    813' .54–dc20   92-44544
                                                          CIP

Printed in Hong Kong

10 9 8 7 6 5 4 3 2 1

Contents

First Snowdrops of Springtime
Sweet whisperings bring,
Of bees, buds and flowers,
And birds on the wing,
All singing one chorus—
Be glad
It is Spring.

ONE

The Legacy

Emaline Madeleine Alexandra McAlister, known as Emma to her family and friends, was very sad indeed. Ever since her beloved grandmother had passed away, she was inconsolable. It was difficult for the family to accept the loss of Nan, and more so for a small girl of eight.

Tender words from her mother fell on deaf ears. Hugs from her father did not stop the ache in her heart. She longed for her namesake, Nana Em. Emma missed the sweet scent of lavender and the cool softness of Nan's graceful hands. Above all, she missed their garden walks and the musical, lilting laughter that had always come so easily for the gracious woman.

"Emma, why don't you come with me to Nan's house?," her mother asked. "I have to pick up a few things from Nan's. Besides, a walk through the garden will do you good."

The tall, slender woman paused at the kitchen door. "Come on, Emma, someone needs to check on Nan's garden — what better person than you?" She looked down at the bowed head of her daughter and smiled at the sight. Wisps of sandy brown hair were beginning to slip from the freshly plaited braids. Already one knee sock was sliding down a thin, bruised and scratched shin. The petticoat had edged itself down and showed beneath the pleated tartan school kilt; the starched white shirt was flaunting its rebellion by hanging out in the back. She sighed, thinking of her mother's death. "God, how I miss Mum. If only she could have stayed longer, for Emma's sake." Aloud she said, "Enough of this. Come on, Emma, let's be off. I really need your help today."

Emma, who had been standing by the kitchen table, dejectedly scuffing her new school oxfords against the metal leg, did not look up. With a deep sigh she walked over to her mother, who hugged her close. Hand in hand they walked out the old screen door and into the beckoning sunshine. It was a hazy summer day, with a tinge of autumn in the air. Nan's house was only three blocks away, but today the walk took longer than usual. It had been a tradition for Emma to stop by each morning on her way to school. It was a time for exploring, for jumping the cracks in the sidewalk, counting blackbirds on the telephone wires, a time for contemplation. Her grandmother would be waiting for her on the spacious verandah, ready for their special time together. The serious little girl would walk with Nan on their daily inspection of the garden and finish off the visit with milk and cookies. In the winter, hot cocoa replaced the milk.

As mother and daughter approached the two-story brick house on Walnut Street, each was lost in thought. They paused at the front gate of the flower-strewn lane and together looked over to the perennial garden on their left. It was hard to believe that Nan would not be there to greet them. The garden had always been her pride and joy, always her private refuge.

"You can work out any problems in a garden," she'd say. "Just dig in the dirt and pull out the weeds from those lovely plants. Pretty soon all your worries will simply melt away. Your reward is a profusion of gorgeous blooms." She would give a mischievous grin and add, "It's also wise to keep the garden fairies happy and to give them a pretty home!"

Emma paused on the first step of the wide verandah and squinted through the curtain of her eyelashes. She could almost see Nan, standing over by the peonies, laughing as she used to, tossing her head to the side and brushing back the wisps that always escaped from the long braid of white hair. Emma shook her head, snapped back to the reality of it all, and walked dejectedly up the stone steps. At the top step, she took her mother's

hand; together they pushed open the squeaking oak door and walked down the cool, dark, mahogany-paneled hall.

A bright shaft of light from the garden room beckoned to them. This was Nan's favorite room, for it overlooked the rambling gardens in the backyard. She had spent many happy hours in this room, surrounded by books and needlework. The old wicker furniture, comfortably worn, was positioned with great care to catch the morning light and the best view of the gardens. Family photographs and trinkets decorated the window sills. A tall wooden artist's easel, balancing an unfinished landscape, stood waiting in a corner.

"Now, Emma, there is something here that Nan wants you to have. Her note says it is in the leather steamer trunk over by her chair." Emma's mother paused at the sight of the old trunk. Nan had inherited it from an eccentric aunt who took pride in being the black sheep of the family. The stickers held great fascination for everyone: Cairo, Paris, Istanbul, Wagga Wagga, Kathmandu, San Francisco, Tonga, Tasmania. They all spoke of great adventure and Nan had made good use of them, weaving stories for all who would listen.

Nan's practical side also put the trunk to good use, for the flat surface provided storage on top as well as inside. Emma's mother busied herself with the job of removing the lamp, two books, a sewing basket, and a pair of reading glasses. She hoped Emma wouldn't see her tears, nor feel her loneliness. Both knelt by the trunk; together they unsnapped the brass clasps and quickly lifted the lid. The scent of lavender and linens wafted up to greet them. Layer upon layer of memories lay silent and beautiful — white upon white, English lace, art work, embroideries, flowers on pillowcases, baby booties, tatted handkerchiefs, it was all there—echoes of a bygone era when life moved more slowly and the gentle arts were important.

Emma's mother spoke first. "Let's see now, Nan says your gift is at the bottom of the trunk." She leaned forward, lifting and sorting. "Aha! Here it is." She triumphantly heaved up a blue fabric bundle and laid it on the floor. Together they unfolded it. Catching sight of a sparkling fuchsia silk fabric and pulling back an edge, they were greeted by a brilliant array of fabric patches and embellishments. Astounded at the jumble of designs, Emma's eyes were wide with surprised delight.

"Emma, this is Nan's crazy quilt, and she wants you to have it." Her mother leaned on one hand and stroked the velvet border. "It is very special because Nan made it all on her own, right down to the tasseled fringe. This little quilt spans many generations of our family. I remember it well. As a child, Mum would keep us entertained with stories about the different fabrics. She wants you to keep it for her, Emma. You must realize and always remember how much you meant to Nan. She wouldn't give this heirloom to just anyone. In many ways it is the story of our family all sewn up in a beautiful little crazy quilt."

"Can I keep it in my room?"

"Of course you can, dear, but you'll need to take good care of it for Nan. It has such beautiful memories sewn into it. I wish it could talk to us."

Emma, unable to contain herself any longer, swept the quilt up in her arms. "Can I sleep under it tonight? Oh, please, Mama, can I?"

"I'll make an agreement with you, dear. Tonight you can sleep under the crazy quilt, and tomorrow you can choose a special place in the house to hang it. That way we'll have memories of Nan with us every day."

Emma swayed and rocked the little quilt in her arms. She looked down in wonder at the bright colors. The silk embroidery glistened and the glass beads caught the morning light, making little rainbows dance on her hands.

The beautiful fabrics were embellished with floral embroideries and elaborate buttons. In many places initials and dates stood out in satin stitches. Emma was startled to see her own name and birthdate done up in fuchsia thread on pale green satin. Every color from Nan's garden was echoed in the little quilt. It was a treasure of beautiful memories, filling Emma with wonder and delight. To think that Nan would trust her with such a beautiful thing! Tears sprang to Emma's eyes, and she clutched the quilt to her chest. Why, it looked like Nan's flower garden and, yes, it even looked like Nan!

TWO

The Rainbow Bridge

Emma solemnly climbed into her feather bed and her mother gently laid the jeweled crazy quilt over her, lovingly tucking the fringed edge under her chin. "Sweet dreams, Emma." She wished Nan could see her granddaughter, lying so still and so somber. The little quilt resembled a brilliant memory map draped over Emma's slender form.

After a kiss from her mother and the nightly blessing, Emma lay very still, as though any movement would bother the little quilt. Cautiously, one hand stole its way up to the quilt's edge. Soon little fingers were twisting and curling the tasseled fringe. Oh, how she missed Nana Em! She had never felt so lost and afraid. A tear slid down her cheek and blotted into the edge of the crazy quilt. She just knew nothing would ever be the same without Nan.

Emma lay very still; slowly, slowly, she drifted off to a dreamland that seemed different from the usual soft, peaceful darkness.

Emma felt a sense of wonder and confusion, for she seemed to be drifting in the air; why, she could almost fly! There, arcing up from her bed, through the ceiling and into the clouds, was a beautiful rainbow bridge! Emma, floating about her bedroom, slowly made her way over to the radiating colors. Her feet sank into the colors but, to her amazement, the bridge supported her weight! Emma ventured a few steps up the rainbow bridge. The colors seemed to spring up at each step, bouncing her along. As Emma looked back, she could see herself, still sound asleep under the crazy quilt. It was wonderful! She had just turned back to concentrate on the colors when she heard the laughter. Emma peered up into the clouds and there, very faintly, she could make out the garden and Nan's house! Could it be possible? There was Nan, over in the garden! And, wonder of wonders, the little jeweled quilt was floating over the walkway near the day-lily beds!

Emma, now a wee bit frightened, hesitated and started back. Looking down, she could see herself sound asleep, so still and so peaceful. Should she go on, or should she return to the safety of her room? She turned again, peering up the rainbow bridge. Yes, for certain, there was Nan! Her beloved grandmother was standing in the garden, waving a wide-brimmed straw hat in greeting. She could hear the familiar voice calling, "Come on up, Emma! You'll be fine, dear. I'm waiting for you!"

Picking up the edge of her long white nightgown, Emma began to run; the rainbow colors, springing up under her feet, sped her along. Soon she was on the garden path. She ran excitedly along, past the hollyhocks and the old, elegant peonies. The Johnny-jump-ups looked on in wide-eyed amazement as the little girl raced by. She ran breathlessly into her grandmother's outstretched arms. How wonderful it was to smell the lavender that was Nan and to feel the warmth of her arms!

"Oh, Emma, my dearest Emma. You've been through such a lot, haven't you? I am so sorry, little one. Now let me look at you. Why, you've grown an inch or more!" Nan stood back, admiring the little girl. "We've been granted this special time together, and I want you to come with me on a tour of the garden."

Gripping the little girl's hand and bending close, Nan began a wondrous story. "I see you have chosen to sleep under my crazy quilt. Oh, the memories it holds for me, Emma, and the understanding it will bring to you!" Nan smiled down at her granddaughter and stopped on the path. "What it lacks in size, it makes up in color and memories." The crazy quilt danced and weaved in front of them as if trying to show off.

"I was such a gangly child, so shy and

awkward. My mother grew quite worried about my lack of co-ordination. But Father always said, 'Relax, Mother, she's but a wee small filly, a real thoroughbred. You'll see!' I loved him for that!" Nan looked down at Emma's upturned face, the replica of her childhood form, and sighed.

"You're the same, Emma. One day you'll be greatly admired for your grace and beauty. As father always said, 'Good horses need to stumble about on wobbly legs before they can run free. The swan has to be the ugly duckling to know the true meaning of humility.'" She brushed the straggly wisps of hair from her brow and absentmindedly did the same for Emma.

Emma peeked over her grandmother's arm and down the rainbow bridge. Amazingly, there she was, sleeping peacefully under the crazy quilt; yet, when she turned her head, she saw the dazzling little quilt floating over the garden path! "So much for the wonder of a dream," she thought matter-of-factly. She was without fear or worries, for she was with her beloved Nan. She felt safe and happy for the first time in many days. Everything remained as it had been before Nan's sudden departure.

"Do you see that small blue patch in the left lower corner, Emma?" Nan pointed to the dancing quilt, which now hovered over the columbines. "This piece is from my school pinafore. Mother had to mend it regularly, as I kept tearing it on the bramble bushes behind our house. I lost more hair ribbons there! I like to think the robins used them to decorate their nests. What do you think, Emma?" Her hand reached down to stroke the little girl's hair. She added wistfully, "I really detested that school uniform, Emma. It was so ugly and old-fashioned. I longed to wear something sophisticated like Mother would wear."

The quilt slowly floated towards them and Nan gasped with pleasure, "Look! Here's a piece of Mother's rose silk evening dress! Emma, how I wish you could have known your great-grandmother. She was exactly like this fabric — warm, vibrant, and so elegant. Mother wore her hair in a mass of loose curls high upon her head and Father loved buying pretty combs for her! He was so proud of her. He had two terms of endearment for Mother: 'Lady Lillian' among their friends, and 'Lillikins' at home. Mother looked for the best in people and could draw out the shyest type. Because of her, the house was full of music and laughter. She had a witty sense of humor that always entertained but never ridiculed — something we should all remember!"

They began to walk, past the purple loosestrife and the Shasta daisies, towards the backyard. The little quilt danced and twirled ahead of them, like a magic carpet of color.

Nan continued, "Sometimes, as my parents took their evening walks in the garden, I would follow and hide behind the shrubs. When they thought they were quite alone, he would carefully remove the combs and her hair would cascade down like a waterfall of auburn curls. I can hear her laughter now. My, how they loved each other!" Nan looked down at her granddaughter's sandy brown hair and smiled at the sight of the red highlights. "It was good to see that love, Emma!"

As they started down the walkway, Nan continued: "Father was very tall and rather quiet. He didn't waste many words, always thinking them over before he spoke. His hair was coal black and his eyes were dark brown. Now that I think of it, he always wore a tweed jacket and a tie. Mother would tease him, and said somewhere in his ancestry a beautiful Gypsy fell in love with an English professor!" Nan laughed at the memory. "I suppose to some people he would seem boring, but beneath that quiet exterior was the most romantic and kindest soul I've ever known.

"He was an unusual man, Emma. He wasn't afraid to show his gentle heart. You'll find, my dear, that it takes more courage to be kind and gentle than it does to be spiteful and rough." She ruffled Emma's hair and laughed, "Besides, it has a lot more rewards!

"Father was a medical doctor and had his practice right here at the house. Mind you, he didn't doctor only people. In the backyard he had a series of small cages along the stable walkway. Here he was doctor and caretaker to all types of little animals. The neighborhood menagerie of budgie birds, cats, dogs, mice, and gerbils were all brought for medical care, not to mention all the wild birds and animals we'd find in the back woods. Mother would scold him when he had more animal patients than people patients. Truth be known, she spent more time out there than he did. Yes, they were a good team, a beautiful blend of opposites."

Nan's attention returned to the quilt. "I put this piece of Harris tweed here, next to Mother's evening dress. It looks right, doesn't it, Emma." It was more of a statement than a question. They stood together on the garden path, both lost in thought, gazing at the two patches, so different and yet blending together as one.

THREE

Teddy Tabby Cat

ook down the rainbow bridge, Emma." Nan's voice was soft and low. "You look so peaceful sleeping under my little quilt." Emma peered down the path and lowered her eyes. It was as though she could see through the ground, giving the illusion that Nan's garden and house were floating on a see-through cloud.

"Can you see that lovely piece of white lace, right up near the top, just below your chin?"

Emma, solemnly nodding yes, leaned forward for a better view. Nan began to chuckle, bursting into a childish giggle. "That fabric is from my brother Harrison's christening gown. Mother made it before he was born. I think she was expecting him to be a girl. That gown was all lacy, with tucks, ruffles, scads of pink and blue bows, and rows of little seed pearls. Luckily, Harrison was quite oblivious when he wore it! Mother always said I looked much better in it!"

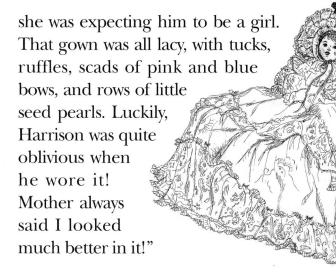

Together they sat on the stone bench nestled among the potentilla shrubs. "My goodness, but Harrison was a rascal. He delighted in being the elder child and caused me more grief than I care to remember. I was the perfect target for his pranks and endless teasing. Why, it's a wonder I survived!

"This patch of christening gown brings back many memories. Mother kept it wrapped in tissue and scented with sprigs of lavender, tucked among her many treasures in the linen closet. You should have seen that linen closet, Emma. It was in a dark hallway off the bedrooms, behind two huge mahogany doors.

There were floor-to-ceiling shelves stacked with linens, all arranged more carefully than a library. I loved to stand on the wooden ladder and help Mother put things away.

"In those days, I always played with my dolls and a lovely tabby cat named Teddy. He was such a patient old dear. I dressed him up in doll clothes and pushed him about in a wicker baby carriage." She chuckled at the memories. "He endured all of this with great dignity. In fact, we loved him so much that Father asked a photographer to take his picture. Mother made Teddy a silk bow for the occasion and we all stood by while the photographer fussed with his equipment. In those days a photograph took forever. The subject had to sit perfectly still for ever so long. Can you imagine? That lovely old cat, sitting patiently, with all of us giving encouragement from the sidelines. He must have truly loved us, to put up with such nonsense.

"One day I was looking through Mother's linen closet and I spied the christening gown. It was too much of a temptation, and besides I'd become terribly bored with my doll clothes. Before I knew it, I was rushing out of the house with Teddy sitting upright in the carriage, his eyes all squinty with humiliation, his ears flattened back under the ridiculous lace hat! The christening gown was buttoned up and bunched under his back legs. Poor old Teddy!"

She wiped a tear from her eye. "I raced down the backyard path, careened around the corner and — there was Harrison, pedaling furiously towards us on his bike! I just froze and he frantically tried to brake. There was a profusion of great, loud shouts and screams as we collided! In my confusion, I fell down, still gripping the carriage handle. Teddy catapulted through the air, like a circus springboard act! Harrison's shouts and accusations turned to wide-eyed amazement, and he just lay there watching as Teddy sailed through the air, the christening gown billowing about him like a dainty, tubular parachute!"

Nan's shoulders began to shake with laughter and her words came in gasps. "The little bonnet had slipped over his eyes. His feet were wide apart and his tail was bushed out in stark fear. He crashed into the big dogwood bush, just missing the fish pond! All we could hear were hideous yowls and snarls as bits of the gown began to float to the ground. I was absolutely horrified, not believing my eyes. The sudden silence made me move. Do you know, Emma, all I found in that bush were jagged bits of christening gown. No bonnet, and no Teddy! The poor old dear didn't come home for three days, and then minus the bonnet!

"That terrible brother of mine just hooted with laughter. He proceeded to prance about and made me even more miserable, as he went on about my sure fate with Mother. As I frantically tried to collect the bits and pieces of christening gown, Harrison began a chant:

'You'll be torn to shreds, bit by bit,
You'll be spanked on the bottom till you
    can't sit;
Off in the background you'll be hearing
The voice of Harrison, cheering and cheering.'

With those last words, he'd whoop and holler with delight. He could hardly wait to tell Mother. I remember my tears as he raced off ahead. I searched through the bushes and gathered up the remains of that beautiful gown. The last piece was floating like a torn sail atop Harrison's boat in the fish pond. I was in such despair that I just waded in without taking off my shoes! Then I trudged slowly back to the house, resigned to whatever punishment fate dealt me. There was Mother standing on the porch, arms folded and foot tapping; Harrison gloated triumphantly at her side. It was the longest few yards I've ever had to walk.

"I was severely reprimanded and confined to my room for a week—but so was Harrison! He protested at great lengths, but Mother held firm. She didn't appreciate the way he gloated in my misery. She also informed him that, as the elder, he was responsible for me."

Nan shrugged her shoulders. "I felt a bit guilty about Harrison's punishment but," her eyes twinkled, "then again, not that bad! It made up for all the pranks he played on me." She chuckled, "Being the elder child does have some drawbacks at times. Harrison always complained that he had to set the examples that I never followed. Ah, well, it was a marvelous childhood, nevertheless!"

Emma mulled over Nan's words. "Well, I suppose he was right, Nan, but being an only child is worse. I'd give anything for a big brother, even a mean one. And, as you know, Nan..." Her words trailed off, and her eyes grew round and questioning.

From out of the potentilla shrubs, just beside Nan, a large tabby cat strolled slowly to the walkway. He sat down directly in front of them and proceeded to indulge in a methodical cat bath. He thoroughly licked his left front paw and rubbed behind his left ear; he had just begun on the right side when Nan broke the silence: "My dear Emma, permit me to introduce you to Teddy Tabby Cat, my dear friend and constant companion. He was the first to greet me when I passed to this world."

In response to this grand introduction, Teddy stood up, yawned a big contented meow, and strolled over to Emma. She could hardly catch her breath, she was so amazed. The little girl haltingly reached out her hand. Sure enough, he was real and felt very well fed at that! She began to stroke his back and he greeted her with a deep rumbly purr, his eyes squinting with pleasure as she scratched behind his ears.

Nan stood up. "Let's be off, Emma; there's so much more I want to tell you." Turning to the cat, she said, "Come along Teddy. You can be our escort." Strolling hand in hand, they started down the walkway. The large cat followed closely behind, massive head held high, eyes alert and tail bristling with annoyance at the bouncy, glittering crazy quilt that swooped and dived at him like a mother magpie! Ah, the indignities of life to be endured by gentlemen tabby cats.

FOUR

The Enchanted Garden

Nan stooped over the old red geranium to snap off the last spent flower. Emma, enjoying the comfortably familiar scene, was lying on the prickly green carpet of lawn.

"Nan, I've been thinking about your brother. Was it really that bad — having an older brother, I mean?"

Nan laughed and walked over to her granddaughter. Sitting down beside Emma, she hugged her knees close. "Now don't get me wrong, dear. Harrison was a wonderful brother. I suppose you could describe living with him as character building!"

"Oh, Nan! Was it really that bad?"

"No, dear, truly it wasn't. Many times Harrison proved to be a dear brother. When I was your age, he really proved to be my hero."

Emma squirmed with delight at the prospect of another story.

Nan continued, "I played every day in the gardens. One day I was half asleep on the lawn over by the fish pond. A large blue dragonfly landed near my hand. I kept ever so still, watching it, when I heard a tiny voice call out, 'Dragonfly, dragonfly, come to me!'

"I couldn't believe my ears, but it called again, 'Dragonfly, dragonfly, come to me. Stay as still as still can be.' From out of the tall grass a tiny figure appeared. It was a garden fairy with gossamer wings and a silvery gown. She had long, flowing blond hair and wore a garland of foxglove blossoms. I'm sure she was a fairy princess, because she was so beautiful! The dragonfly rose up and, gliding over to the fairy, hovered while she seated herself on its back. In the blink of an eye they were gone.

"At the time, I thought it was a dream; but, after that, I began to see many other fairies in the garden. There were baby fairies, lady fairies, and even gentleman fairies. They all lived in the flower blossoms and under the fern fronds. The baby fairies were my favorites: I'd find them asleep in the honeysuckle, cradled in a leaf with the blossoms for shade. They were completely naked except for wood-violet hats and sheer organdy wings. The honeybees stood guard and serenaded them with droning lullabies. It was lovely to see! I told my family about the fairies, and everyone but Harrison believed me.

"I went off to school and told my teacher about the fairies. My one mistake was telling her in front of the class. I was greeted with whoops of laughter. A group of older girls, headed by the teacher's pet, Mabel Dawson, took it upon themselves to tease me about the garden fairies. They were merciless and I was miserable. I decided to invite them to our garden to see for themselves. Little did I know that only true believers can see the fairies, and that they live only in true believers' gardens.

"On the following Saturday they all showed up. Mabel sniggered, 'So where are all the fairies, Em?'

'Follow me and I'll show you, but please be very quiet.'

'Of course,' she sneered. 'We'll do that, won't we, girls?'

They all chimed in, 'Of course, of course!'

"We trooped to the back garden, where I proceeded to point out the little fairies among the flowers. Mabel suddenly snapped, 'Look, Em, this is absolutely ridiculous. There is no such thing as a fairy. You are a liar!'

"A voice from the open sun-room window called down, 'But you're wrong, Mabel Dawson. There are fairies in this garden. I've seen them myself!' We all turned to look up, and there was Harrison, grinning down at us. For once, Mabel was speechless. She had a huge crush on Harrison and he wouldn't give her the time of day. Now she found herself in quite a dilemma: here was the object of her adoration, claiming he saw the garden fairies.

"By now, Harrison had sauntered out to the backyard. All the girls started to giggle and flutter about. I'd never seen such a performance. Mabel was the first to speak. 'Harrison, surely you don't believe in such nonsense?'

"He looked over to me, winked, and said, 'Of course I do — and Em has shown them to me. I see them all the time. Why, Mabel Dawson, can't you see the fairy sitting on my shoulder?'

"He leaned his left shoulder toward the girls. All eyes, including my own, were riveted to his shoulder. Mabel, sensing a prime opportunity, exclaimed, 'Why, yes, I do see the fairy, I really do!' All the girls agreed and ooh-ed and aah-ed over Harrison's invisible fairy.

"I looked and looked again, but I could not see the fairy, even though I was a true believer! But I did have the presence of mind to keep quiet. Harrison proceeded to strut about as if the fairy were riding on his shoulder. It was a fine performance. Finally they left, all twittering on about Harrison's garden fairy.

"We stood together at the gate and waved goodbye to the girls. As they turned the corner, Harrison turned to me and glared. 'Well, I saved you this time, Sis, but don't expect it to happen again. I did this just to make a fool out of that pesky Mabel Dawson. You and your stupid garden fairies!'

"I was about to thank him when a radiant light appeared on Harrison's left shoulder. There sat the queen of the garden fairies, nestled close to his shirt collar, waving and blowing kisses to me. She was gorgeous: her silvery hair was sprinkled with freesia blossoms; her gown was iridescent green feathers with a cobweb train. She wore diamond slippers and rings on every finger. Fairy dust fluttered from her wings.

"I tried hard to listen to Harrison's words. After all, he had just rescued me from Mabel Dawson. But my eyes kept returning to the smiling fairy. I tried to distract him with a big hug and a muffled 'I love you!'

"His answer to that was, 'I love you, too, you little pest. Now forget those silly fairy stories.' Off he went, with the queen of the garden fairies still waving and blowing kisses from his shoulder!"

Emma was entranced by the story. "Nana Em, that was wonderful. Do you think I'll ever see a garden fairy?"

"You have to believe with all your heart, and you have to love flowers. That's why I added the dragonflies and flower embroideries to my quilt. Do you like them, dear?"

"Oh yes, Nan, they are so pretty, but I do wish I could see the garden fairies."

"Close your eyes and think of the fairies, Emma; welcome them into your heart."

The little girl stood up, closed her eyes, wrinkled her nose in concentration, and clasped her hands to her chest. "I do believe, truly I do." The quilt floated over her as she repeated, "I truly do believe." She paused, concentrating on fairies.

The silence was broken by a little reedy voice, singing,

> "Dragonfly, dragonfly, come to me.
> Stay as still as still can be.
> Dragonfly, dragonfly, can't you see,
> We don't need reality.
> Dragonfly, dragonfly, ride out to sea;
> Let us greet eternity."

At that, Emma tentatively opened one eye and the other eye quickly flew open in amazement. "Welcome to our garden, dear Emma." Hovering at eye level was the beautiful fairy queen. She was just as Nan had described. She rode sidesaddle upon a large monarch butterfly, her feather gown gently cascading off to the side. Directly behind her was a fairy princess, riding upon a large, iridescent dragonfly, who darted about impatiently and tugged at the silver reins. They raised their right hands in unison and blew a kiss to the little girl. The cloud of fairy dust made her blink, and she could hear the sound of laughter. As they flew away, the tiny princess turned the dragonfly around, waved, and called out, "Goodbye, little Emma. You are a true believer after all."

First Love

henever the crazy quilt bobbed in front of Nan and Emma, the sun would flash upon a gold fabric, causing light rays to twinkle on the path. Emma skipped about, trying to step on the lights; but they escaped her every try. Skip, hop, skip, hop.

"Nan, what is that fabric trying to do? Why, it's almost laughing at me!"

Nan's eyes grew soft and dreamy. "No, my dear, it's telling us it loves us. That fabric is from my very first grown-up gown. Mother finally relented and made me a dress just like hers. I was seventeen and so impressionable. Harrison had been invited to a very posh afternoon party over in Oldborough. He took me along, more as a favor to Mother, really. I was so nervous and unsure of myself. My shoes had lovely bows and high heels, but I was rather wobbly and Harrison added to my misery by calling me 'Wiggles'! I felt so out of place. When we arrived, several of Harrison's classmates rushed up, boisterous and rough, completely ignoring me. Emma, I can feel the panic even now. I wanted to bolt and run. Instead, I just stood there, trying to act as if I didn't care. Then one of them turned to me and said, 'Hello'! Just like that, a simple hello. I was struck dumb — for he was simply the most beautiful boy I had ever laid eyes on. I can't remember another word he said or how I acted.

"His name was John Penn. A Canadian from Toronto, he had large brown eyes and curly black hair that never stayed in place. John was quite tall and lean, with lovely long legs. He had a shy way of tilting his head to one side when he laughed. I was madly in love from that minute on. Harrison thought John was daft when he offered to walk about the party with me! I just floated on those high heels, Emma, I really did! It turned out to be a glorious afternoon and the beginning of a beautiful romance."

Nan paused to stare out into the back garden, one hand slowly brushing the wisp of hair from her eyes. "From that moment on, John found lots of excuses to come to our house. Harrison was completely dumbfounded by it all. He couldn't understand what John saw in me! Here was one of his best friends, more interested in his little sister than in hanging about with the boys!"

She paused, smiling down at the little girl. "Do you know what he saw, Emma?"

The braided head shook a serious no.

"Why, he saw the swan, Emma, where Harrison saw only the ugly duckling. John saw a beautiful young woman. I felt cherished because of what I saw mirrored in his eyes. Do you understand, darling?"

"Well, I think I do, Nan," Emma stopped and pondered. "Do you remember my horse

Dusty, Nan? He used to belong to Mama when she was a girl. I guess it's something like my horse Dusty. He's very old, Nan, and when you pet him, dust flies up. I try so hard to keep him clean. That's not how he got his name, you know; Mother named him Dusty because of his brindled color. Some of my friends tease me and say he's an old flea bag. But I look into his eyes and they're so trusting and he loves me. I don't see an old horse; I just see my beautiful, faithful friend. When we're together, I call him 'Kentucky Blue Grass' and I'm sure it makes him feel better. He's really very beautiful to me! So, I guess it's sort of like that?"

As Emma paused to catch her breath, Nan bent down and hugged the little girl to her. "Yes, my dear, it's something like that. Beauty is truly in the eyes of the beholder!"

"Tell me more about John," Emma pleaded.

"Well, let's see. Mother and Father were quite marvelous with John. We must have reminded them of when they first met, and I think they relived the wonder of it all. That was the most beautiful summer of my life, and I wore the gold dress many times. I danced in my high-heeled shoes till I wore them out! When we weren't dancing, we were talking. That was a special quality in John: he listened as well as he talked. He was at our house every day, and even Harrison got used to the idea of sharing his friend with me!"

Emma looked up into her grandmother's thoughtful blue eyes. "But, Nan," she squeaked, "Grandpa's name was Douglas."

Nan smiled down and nodded. "Yes indeed, and I loved him with all my heart, but that was much later, dear." She went on, "John was my first love. And, no matter your age, you never forget the wonder of that first love."

"But Nan, if you loved John so much, why didn't he become my grandpa?"

"Well, darling, it was the summer of 1914

and the war was stirring in Europe. Harrison and John enlisted. They were so proud of themselves! I remember the look of terror on my mother's face when they marched home to tell us. My heart simply stopped beating and I could barely hear their voices. Father just sat there, sad and very quiet, yet he was proud of them, too.

"The boys had three weeks before they reported for duty. Everyone was determined to make it three weeks of memories. We partied every night with our friends, visited all the relatives, took long walks and, above all else, we discussed our futures. He was going to be an important politician, maybe become prime minister. I was going to be his helpmate, and a famous artist on the side." She sighed and looked over to her granddaughter. "We were so young and we had such hopes. Most of our plans were made right here in this garden.

"The departure day arrived all too soon. I'll never forget the feeling of hopelessness as we saw them off at the train station. Everyone was trying to be so cheerful and brave." Nan's voice faded to a whisper and a big sigh pushed out the words. "The truth is, Emma, Harrison came home and John did not. We were informed of his death the last week of the war. He was buried with countless others in Flanders Field in Belgium. It was so far away. I've always grown these poppies in his memory." She stooped to point out the orange and red poppies along the walkway.

"I thought my world had ended with his death and, once again, Harrison came through for me. He didn't leave my side for a year. He was always there for me. When I thought I couldn't go on, he'd say, 'John gave us all such happiness. Why cloud the memories with endless grief?' He would take me for long evening walks, and he even helped me with the garden. That year my brother became my friend.

"Mother and Father were wonderful to me, and so patient. They knew it would take time. It was Mother who suggested that I work out my sorrow in this little quilt. She started me off with the piece from her favorite rose-colored dress. Soon everyone was contributing to this memory quilt. Seeing it grow helped them all, and it helped me to heal. Slowly, month by month, John's voice began to fade. After two or three years, I would sometimes forget what he looked like. God, I felt so guilty about that...."

Emma was very quiet as she studied the little poppies and the crazy quilt floating above them. "Do you ever see him in this magic garden, Nan?"

Nan walked over to the willow chair by the birdbath and sat down. Looking up at her granddaughter, she smiled and nodded her head, confirming what Emma hoped would be "Yes." As Nan gazed off, lost in her special thoughts, the crazy quilt floated slowly towards her and gently folded itself over her lap. Four bronze military buttons caught the sunrays and Nan's hand rested on a khaki green square of Army serge.

SIX

Pop! Goes the Weasel

an bent over and picked a weed from the border of pansies lining the walkway. The cheerful orange and gold flower faces were framed with petal frills of purple. "Have you ever seen colors like these, Emma?"

The little girl grinned up at her grandmother. The question was like a game to her. Ever since she could remember, her grandmother asked the same question each time she looked at the colorful little pansies. No answer was expected. "I think they are simply the pretties pansies I've ever seen," Nan exclaimed. "Every time I look at them I remember my first little garden.

"All through my childhood we had a wonderful old gardener named Claude. He was of a mixed Negro and Indian heritage. He claimed he was of the Heinz 57 tribe. Claude thought this was very amusing, and he'd laugh at his own joke. I loved him so much; he was my special friend. Claude lived on the edge of town in an old wooden shanty, and out front little pansies grew everywhere. Each morning we would pass each other, I on my way to school and Claude on his way to work. He would sweep the hat off his head and bow very low. I always replied with a curtsy. We'd laugh and visit for a few minutes, then go on with our day. He always made me feel like a real lady.

"He was such a dignified gentleman, over six feet tall and slim. He carried himself very erect; the old faded shirt and overalls never took away from his dignity. Claude had a wiry, curly head of white hair on which he wore an old African pith helmet. In his knapsack he carried a beat-up ancient violin which he played night and day, all kinds of plaintive songs and lots of jigs. His pride and joy was an old burl walnut pipe. When it wasn't nesting in the front pocket of his bib overalls, it hung from his mouth on the left side." Nan paused, "Come to think of it, his bottom tooth was worn short because of it!

"Mother always invited him in for lunch when he worked in our yard, but he insisted on eating in the back garden under the oak tree. When he finished eating, he'd play the fiddle. I often joined him, dancing to the music and listening to wonderful stories about his childhood. After the stories, he would reach into his knapsack and produce a big red apple or a juicy orange, which he would share with me. Around Christmas time, it would be stick candy or a pretty hair ribbon. He was always so kind."

Nan shook her head. "Do you know, Emma, I was fourteen years old before I even realized his skin was a different color than mine?"

The little quilt bobbed over the pansies and then drifted closer to Emma and Nan. Nan squinted in the sun as she concentrated on the crazy quilt. "Look over here, Emma," she demanded, pointing to a rectangular piece of lilac silk. "Claude gave me this cigarette silk for my crazy quilt when I was a young woman. They were giveaways in cigarette and cigar packets. The silks were decorated with pictures of famous actors and actresses, cowboys, Indians, even plants and animals. They were very popular collectibles then."

Emma peered closely at the lilac silk. Painted in the center was a beautiful woman wearing a garland of pansies and a haunting smile. "She's lovely, isn't she? Her name was Ethel Green and she was a famous actress when I was your age." Nan turned back to the pansies.

"Claude started me on my very first garden. It was just a three-foot square over here behind the pansies. I can still see it when I close my eyes. A jumble of Shasta daisies, a little patch of snapdragons, a single sunflower towering in the back, and these little purple and orange pansies in the front. Claude gave them to me as a special gift from his garden. You know, they are called 'Jolly Jokers,' a truly appropriate name for such a cheerful little flower.

"That little garden gave me such pleasure. Claude would smile and say, 'Too bad people can't learn to live in harmony like your flowers do. Just look at all them colors, all different, yet they're harmonized into one pretty little garden. Yep, they're lucky they got old Mother Earth holdin' them close and Father

Sky watchin' over them.' He'd play a jig on his fiddle and I would curtsy and dance for the little flowers in my garden." Nan's voice drifted off as she gazed beyond the pansies. The faint sound of a violin could be heard.

Emma turned and looked to where her grandmother's attention was drawn. Over near the sunflowers stood a stately old gentleman, swaying to the music of the fiddle tucked under his chin. He looked towards the two and bowed very low, the fiddle and bow clasped to his chest, the other hand sweeping the old pith helmet close to the ground. Nan clasped her hands in delight and returned a low, graceful curtsy. Claude started a new song and the little crazy quilt began to rock and sway to the music. Emma could feel her toes tingle, and soon her feet were skipping to the beat of the fiddle. The little pansies nodded and bobbed with delight. Nan clapped her hands and her feet tapped in time. No longer able to keep still, she turned to the little crazy quilt and caught hold of a corner. Turning to Emma, she grasped her hand, and all together they danced in a circle with Claude. Laughter filled the garden as he played the old musical jig:

"A penny for a ball of thread,
Another for a needle.
That's the way the money goes;
POP! goes the weasel!

All around the cobbler's bench
The monkey chased the people;
The monkey thought 'twas all in fun.
POP! goes the weasel!"

The musical beat got faster and faster. The dancers separated from the circle and moved about the lawn. Claude danced in place, concentrating on the tempo. The little quilt swooped and dived:

"Queen Victoria's very sick;
Napoleon's got the measles;
Sally's got the whooping cough;
POP! goes the weasel!

Of all the dances ever planned
To fling the heel and fly the hand,
There's none that proves so gay and grand
As POP! goes the weasel!"

With the final "POP!" they all fell down,

laughing and giggling. The little quilt danced excitedly in the midst of them all.

"Oh, Claude, thank you for that wonderful dance!," Nan exclaimed. "It was just like old times, except I fell down more gracefully in the old days!" She reached for her straw hat, which had tumbled into the flower bed, then smoothed back her hair.

"It was my pleasure, Miss Em." The old gentleman rose to his feet and helped Nana Em to hers. "You can still dance a mighty fine jig!" Turning to the little girl, he held out his hand. "It's a true pleasure to meet you, little Emma; you're the spittin' image of your grandmother. I can see you're going to be a real beauty." Emma stretched to grasp the old gentleman's hand and, with one strong pull, she was on her feet.

Claude swung the worn canvas knapsack from his back and began to search through the side pocket. "Now, let's see what we have in here for such a pretty young lady." His kind eyes twinkled. "Aha! Here it is!" He reached his hand out to Emma and dropped a blue hair ribbon onto her outstretched palm.

Emma smiled up at him as she curtsied low. Claude bowed in return. "Oh, thank you, Mr. Claude. It's such a pleasure to meet you. Truly it is!" Nana Em was right; she felt like a real lady.

My love is in this
Your heart
chains to

For Auld
Lang Syne
Hearty Wishes
for a guid New Year
From

SEVEN

"That Lydia!"

alking to the very back of the garden, Nan and Emma stopped to view the rose garden. It was carefully manicured, so different from the wild cottage garden along the sides. All the rosebushes were spaced in symmetrical lines; white pebbles covered the ground. Every rose was red or white except for one in the middle, which was a deep, purplish black, standing out above all the others, with long, elegant stems and dark, shiny leaves. The crazy quilt, which had been swaying about in front of them, darted over to the unusual rosebush and hovered above it.

"Oh, yes!," Nan exclaimed. "My dear Aunt Lydia! Emma, there was a woman who lived before her time. She was Father's only sister,

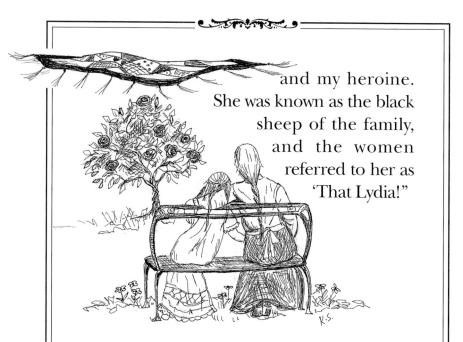

and my heroine. She was known as the black sheep of the family, and the women referred to her as 'That Lydia!'"

Nan smiled at the memory. "How I envied her! I wanted to be just like her when I grew up. But somehow I always gave in and did what was expected of me. That's one of my few regrets.

"No matter the occasion, Lydia always stood out in a group. She had a flair for the exotic." Nan settled down on the wrought-iron bench at the left of the roses. Emma, sensing a story, nestled close to her grandmother's side.

"Father and Lydia, being the only children, were extremely close. Everything he did, Lydia tried to do better. He was her hero in life, and she always needed his approval. When Father took up riding, Lydia became a champion jumper, wearing breeches instead of a skirt. When Father took up swimming, so did she. Father loved the classics, so Lydia read them aloud with him. Father played the piano, and Lydia sang opera. And so it went. In many ways, she was his alter ego. Father was so shy and studious; secretly, he delighted in her outrageous nature and free spirit. In trying to be like him, she sometimes managed to outdo him.

"Their mother feared Lydia would never become a lady, so she was sent off at a young age to the Hawthorn Academy for Young Women. Lydia was heartbroken at leaving her brother and rebelled right from the start. She created a stir by piercing her ears and wearing a turban fashioned from her school bloomers! If that wasn't enough, she was caught smoking cigarettes in the attic and making elderberry wine in the cellar! Her parents were summoned to the school more than once.

"The usual punishment was to scrub the

stone hallways after class, with soapy water and a toothbrush. On her father's first visit to the school, he inquired as to Lydia's grades and behavior. The headmistress replied, 'Her grades are superior and the halls of Hawthorn Academy have never been so clean!'

"The final straw was when she ran off to march in a parade for women's rights! Poor Lydia was expelled from school and sent home in disgrace. For Lydia, this was a triumph: she was happy to be back with her brother.

"When my father went off to medical school, Lydia wanted to follow. That's when the boom really fell!"

Nan sighed and shook her head at the memory. "Their father, being of the old

school, forbade her to go. He believed women should be taught only the gentle arts of needlework and homemaking, that university made them difficult and willful. No matter how Lydia pleaded and begged, he would not change his mind. There were terrible scenes, and her brother even threatened to leave medical school.

"Lydia bobbed her hair and went on a hunger strike. She went so far as to tear up all her party gowns. Her father finally said, 'With dramatics like this, you should go off and become an actress.' And so she did! Off she went, in the middle of the night. The next anyone heard, she was performing and singing on Broadway. Her father claimed that he no longer had a daughter, and he forbade her mother to contact her. Lydia was equally as stubborn, and she never returned to this town as long as her father was alive."

Nan stood up, looking wistfully towards the stately rosebush. "It was sad, because they did love each other so very much. What a pity she was ahead of her time and he was so behind! They just could not accept each other's ways."

Turning back to Emma, she went on. "Anyway, my dear, she became an international celebrity. She was a great star and we were in awe of her. She married three times! The first was to a German count who gave her diamonds, the second was to a Spanish prince who left her a castle, and the third was to an American playwright who simply adored her.

"I loved my eccentric aunt and anxiously awaited our annual visit to her. Whenever we went to visit her, Aunt Lydia would let me dress up in her costumes and jewelry. I would walk about in her high heels, and she would encourage me to add more jewelry to my already outrageous costumes. She taught me to sing and to project my voice; it was wonderful! We would act out plays together. She made me feel so special. She always had a little white Persian cat named Sasha with her, as part of the exotic flair. Above all, Aunt Lydia never tired of exploring: we would receive postcards from all parts of the globe.

Why, she even climbed a mountain to visit a monastery in Tibet, and she once sang for a sheik in the Sahara Desert.

"She was very brave, always speaking out for women's rights. She argued for the vote and gave a great deal of money for women's scholarships. She never got over her lack of a university education. She even went so far as to march with the suffragettes and would often be the key speaker at the rallies. People didn't seem to mind, and always forgave her because of her outrageous beauty and wit.

"In Paris she was part of the arty crowd, hob-nobbing with painters and writers. She was prized for her intelligence and charming sense of humor. Who couldn't love Aunt Lydia?

"The only time I ever saw Lydia lower her exotic façade was right after her father's death. She returned from Europe for the funeral. More people came to the funeral to see her than to pay tribute to her father! After the reception, my father showed his sister the scrapbooks, all carefully documenting her theatrical career and escapades. Their father had kept the clippings up-to-date, and yet, through all those years, he had never so much as mentioned her name. That night the sound of her crying kept us all awake."

The crazy quilt swooped down in front of them as if demanding their immediate attention. Rhinestones twinkled from a bright purple cloth. Ostrich feather tips draped from a silver and jet brooch. Embroidered across the bottom were the words "Education = Freedom; Life = Education."

Emma reached up to touch the feather plume, as if trying to connect to Aunt Lydia. Nan shrugged her shoulders, and tears sprang to her eyes. "Let's all be thankful for the Aunt Lydias of the world. God knows we need them.

"When my father and I put in this rose garden, we ordered seven white and eight red roses, all the same type and size. We planted them in three rows of five plants, alternating the colors. We wanted it to look like an estate rose garden. That is exactly what we planted; but, if you count them now, there are seven red and seven white roses. That black rose appeared the year Aunt Lydia died. There it is, right in the center of the middle row. We've always called it Lydia's Rose. It was amazing: for seven years that rosebush was scarlet, but suddenly it grew taller and darker, and the flowers turned to that purplish black. When Father saw it for the first time, he just smiled, shook his head, and said, 'That's Lydia!'"

EIGHT

Shy Violets

Emma stepped off the path and into the garden. Bending over, she studied the wood violets beneath the oak tree. They grew in great profusion, carpeting the bases of the tiger lilies. She picked a small cluster of violets and offered them to her grandmother. Nana Em looked at them closely and, holding them to her nose, sniffed long and deep. "Ah, the scent of violets; what memories it brings!"

She looked down at Emma and smiled. "Emma, if you help me weed this area, I'll tell you all about your Grandfather Douglas. Bring that basket closer. It will hold the weeds."

Together they knelt down, and Nan continued. "I've always been affected by the beauty of plants. By the time I was ten, I had memorized the botanical names of all our garden flowers. It was only natural that I'd try to draw them. Mother sent me off to weekly art lessons at the age of twelve, taught by an elderly spinster named Pansey Pughe who took pride in her genteel upbringing."

Emma, hearing the unusual name, gave a squeal of delight. Nan chuckled. "Honestly, dear, that truly was her given name! From Miss Pughe I learned watercolor techniques, along with pen and ink drawing. I even went so far as to keep a flower journal.

"I met your grandfather when I went away to the art academy. He was a professor there, just over from England and very popular with the male students. I was one of three women students. At the time, Mother and Father were loathe to send me away to the Art Academy. Mother didn't consider art to be a proper education. She wanted me to be a nurse, but Father was more lenient. He was so affected by his sister Lydia's plight that he vowed all his children would receive a good education.

"So, off I went at the tender age of twenty-one. I was terrified at the prospect of leaving home, yet very excited. After settling into a local boarding house, I felt quite homesick!"

She straightened up, brushing back a few wisps of hair. "I met your grandfather on my first day. I was very eager to take my first lesson, which was Free-Form Drawing. Armed with paper, pencils, and lots of hope, I walked into the classroom. Imagine my horror when I looked up: there on the center pedestal was the free form of a naked man! I was frozen to the spot, gasping for breath!

"A gruff British voice called out, 'Well, come in or go out, dear lady; you are disturbing my class!' I pivoted and ran down the hall. Hoots of male laughter followed at my heels. It took several hours for me to regain my composure.

"I went to the local tea room for lunch, and it was very crowded. So I approached an

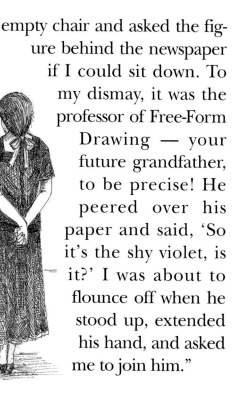

empty chair and asked the figure behind the newspaper if I could sit down. To my dismay, it was the professor of Free-Form Drawing — your future grandfather, to be precise! He peered over his paper and said, 'So it's the shy violet, is it?' I was about to flounce off when he stood up, extended his hand, and asked me to join him."

"Oh! Nan, weren't you embarrassed? I would never have sat down with him."

"To tell the truth, dear, I was in awe of your grandfather. I'd never been around anyone quite like him. He had the presence of a giant. He wore his hair long for those days, and he had piercing blue eyes. His tweed jacket was rumpled, with flecks of paint on the lapel. During our lunch he informed me

he was from Harrowgate, Yorkshire, and that he had been wounded in the war."

Emma gasped. "Oh, poor Grandfather!"

"I'm afraid it wasn't heroic, my dear. One of his own men accidentally shot him in the foot, causing a permanent limp! He always said it was a good excuse to collect silver-handled canes.

"When he asked me what my medium was, I just sat there like a prim and proper Miss Pughe and said, 'Watercolor florals.' He threw back his head and bellowed, 'Flowers? You just paint flowers? Good God, woman, there's more to life than sissy paintings of flowers!' I was furious, and my only response was to jump up and run off once again.

"The next day I was at the door of Free-Form Drawing. I was determined that no one, especially your grandfather, would get the last laugh on me. With head held high, papers clutched to my bosom, eyes straight ahead, I marched over to an empty easel. Gathering all my courage, I looked up at the model. There the young Adonis stood, striking an Olympian pose, draped in a blue sheet! I was amazed, and when I turned to your grandfather he said, 'Welcome, Miss Cameron, to Free-Form Drawing. We all welcome you.' The other students clapped, and not a word was ever mentioned about the blue sheet."

Emma and Nan both smiled and continued plucking at the chickweed. Nan continued, "Father came to visit me and met Professor Hays. Somehow the subject of spring holidays came up, and my teacher was invited for a visit." Nan leaned back on one hand. "Your grandfather was welcomed by everyone. That gruff, grumbly character even went so far as to help me in the garden, all the time muttering about the futility of flowers! The following summer, he rented nearby Haverhill

Cottage and painted vast, sweeping land-scapes. In fact, he rented the cottage for the next four years."

She brushed the soil from her hands and got to her feet. Reaching down, she helped Emma up. Holding the basket between them, they walked toward the house. The lit-tle quilt lingered behind, floating gently over the lilies. Nan looked up to the windows of the sun room.

"I suppose, in the beginning, Douglas was drawn to this house and my family, and I can certainly understand that. It never changed, it was always a constant in my life, a safe haven for all. I returned home after graduat-ing, secure in the bosom of my family. I was employed by the local college to paint and record plants from the Hanford Park area.

"Throughout those summers, I often went with your grandfather on his painting expedi-tions, I with my dainty watercolors and he with his messy tubes of oil paints — all squeezed in the middle."

Emma tugged at her grandmother's sleeve. "So, Nan, when did you get married?"

"Well, it almost didn't happen. After the fifth summer, I realized I was in love with Douglas. No one else mattered; even my memories of John Penn were fading. But Douglas had become more and more distant during that summer. At first I thought it was because he was preparing for an exhibition at the Sandringham Galleries and was engrossed in his work. By the end of the summer, I went to say goodbye. He was overseeing the packing of his canvases and shutting up the cottage.

"As he turned to leave, he saw my tears. I blurted out how much I loved him. I felt such a fool! He sighed and said, 'My dear, shy violet, I'm nineteen years older than you, old enough to be your father. I'm an old wreck, not good for anyone, even for myself. Find yourself a young man and be happy!' With that, he was gone. I was broken-hearted, and even more so when I heard he was returning to England in the fall! Yes, there were lots of young men, but no one like him.

"The following month, Mother and Father escorted me to his art exhibition. The opening was a huge success and every canvas was sold. I was entranced. The massive landscapes were so vibrant and wild! It was incredible to see his work displayed in such prestigious surroundings. It truly was the beginning of his phenomenal career.

"I could see him, off to one side, surrounded by gushing women and rich-looking men. The critics and reporters were hanging on his every word. The lady who owned the gallery was clutching his arm possessively. As usual, he wore his old tweed jacket, his hair was awry, and his tie wasn't done up properly. I noticed that he leaned heavily on his cane as he spoke."

"Nan, weren't you jealous?"

"Well, I must admit to a few pangs of envy! Mother insisted we pay our respects, and we edged our way up to the group. They seemed to be interested in an object to the left of him. I pushed my way to the front and there, on the wall, was a small portrait of a girl holding a posy of violets to her cheek. The nameplate read, 'Shy Violets — Not for Sale.' The girl was me! I stood there in a daze, my mother and father on each side.

"Your grandfather walked over and said, 'Even old fools make mistakes. Could you really put up with me for a few years?' Before I could answer, my mother pushed me forward and said, 'Of course she could, my dear!'

"The rest is history. We were married a month later. Your mother Madeleine arrived the next year; then came Alexandra and Jason.

"We lived in Haverhill Cottage until we moved here to be with Mother. I was very happy with your grandfather. He was absolutely dotty over the children, and they were always with him in the studio. Once in a while he'd paint a floral for me, but he stayed with those sweeping landscapes. He would never admit it, but he loved this garden as much as I."

Nan reached out to stroke Emma's hair. "You may not remember him, Emma, but he was crazy about you. He'd march through the house with you on his shoulders, yelling, 'Here comes Princess Lily!'"

The little quilt floated up the walkway and stopped beside Nan. "Can you see the painted flowers over here?" She pointed out the painted violets and tiger lilies on black velvet. That's your grandfather's little joke. He said that while I appeared to be a shy violet, I was really a tiger lily at heart! I wonder what he meant by that?" Her eyes twinkled mischievously as she smiled down at her granddaughter.

"Now, Nan, how would I know?" They burst into laughter and started up the steps to the sun room. A figure waved to them from the window. Emma, catching sight of the familiar form, ran forward. Nan called after her, "Oh, Emma, just wait till Grandpa Douglas sees his Princess Lily!"

REAL PHOTO
POST CARD

—NINE—

McTavish, Wee Doggie

Nan and Emma made their way along the garden path to the side of the house. In the shade of the north wall, lady-slippers were blossoming among the lacy ferns. It was a calm, mysterious area, dappled by spots of sun filtering through the tall birch tree.

Emma stopped at the water spigot jutting out from the wall. It was a most unusual brass spigot, with two nozzles. The large handle was in the shape of a collie. Nan paused as the child reached for the handle and a cool drink of spring water. "I never pass this area without thinking of McTavish and Lady. Have I told you about them?"

Emma looked up. "Well, I've heard lots of stories about McTavish. He belonged to Mama, didn't he?"

"Actually, he was a gift from me to your grandfather, but the little rascal adopted your mother. So I suppose he did belong to her, certainly in heart and spirit."

"Who was Lady, Nana? I've never heard Mama speak of her."

"I'm not surprised. Your mother has always been a very private person; she keeps things bottled up. Lady was a beautiful sorrel mare who looked just like her name — a real lady. She was given to your mother when she was twelve years old and the mare was a yearling. They were inseparable, and everywhere they went, McTavish was sure to follow. I only have to shut my eyes, and I can see them.

"Now, Emma, I'm getting ahead of myself. Let's water this area while I tell you the story of McTavish."

She turned to the spigot, snapped the hose

in place, and began: "As I said, McTavish was my gift to Grandpa Douglas. He was raised in Yorkshire, you remember, and often he would get quite homesick for the Dales. He told us marvelous stories about the heather-covered hills, the tough Yorkshire farmers, the rugged little sheep, and the hard-working border collies that slink about like shadows. He always reminisced so about the dogs. He gave this puppy the official name of 'McTavish, Wee Doggie.'

"McTavish came from Angus Burns, an old Scotsman who raised sheep over in the Brookshire area. He was a tiny, wizened old man, a bachelor till the day he died. He didn't like people at all, but he did love sheep and border collies.

"McTavish arrived in time for Christmas, and it took him exactly two minutes to charm everyone. That is, everyone except your mother. There he was, a black and white roly-poly ball of mischief with a cold, wet nose. The red bow on his neck lasted about ten seconds, and he wiggled and licked his way through Alexandra, Jason, Grandpa Douglas, and me. We were silly over him; but, try as he would, he couldn't charm Madeleine!"

"I can't understand it, Nan. Mama loves animals. We have oodles of pets because of her." Emma looked up at her grandmother. "Why on earth wouldn't she like such a sweet dog?"

"Believe it or not, your mother was quite unpredictable and moody, especially in her early teens. Sometimes she was jealous of attention given to others."

Emma looked up in amazement. "Are you talking about my Mama? Why, I can hardly believe that, Nan! She's ever so nice to everyone."

Nan shrugged and smiled. "Raising children is quite difficult at times. Your mother is my eldest and so much like me. She was very introverted, very private and far too sensitive. She had so little confidence in herself. She thought she was ugly and that no

one liked her — all those silly teen-age thoughts that we all have." She glanced down at Emma. "Do you know what I mean?" Emma dipped her head and murmured, "I guess so; but gee, Nana, I never thought my mother had those kinds of feelings. Look at her now!"

"Yes, she's like a beautiful swan, isn't she? She's a wonderful woman and a lovely daughter. I'm so proud of her, and she's such a good mother to you.

"In those days she seemed to envy the attention we were giving to the little dog. The more she ignored him, the more determined he became. McTavish became her shadow. He tried everything: puppy whines, wiggles, wet kisses, sad looks; but it all won him little notice.

"In the spring, McTavish ventured outdoors and began following Madeleine on her daily chores. We kept a goat in the horse stable, a few chickens, and two horses: your mother tended them all.

"It was her job to milk Matilda, the nanny goat. This nanny was the meanest, nastiest old goat in history. She just wanted to be left alone. Nothing was safe, as she ate everything in sight. Her favorite game was lying in wait for unsuspecting visitors to the stable. The minute they entered the door, she would charge and knock them over! Only your mother could handle her, although she was only twelve years old at the time. I was terrified of that silly goat and too tender-hearted to get rid of her — and she knew it!

"McTavish took to following your mother to the stable. I happened to be out in the rose garden one morning: that's when I saw McTavish win your mother over. Madeleine walked out of the stable with the nanny goat firmly in hand, and the puppy was bouncing about behind them. She tied the nanny to the poplar tree; all the time the goat was bleating and trying to break loose.

"Madeleine picked up the milk bucket and banged the goat on the head. For about two minutes, the goat stood still. Quick as a flash, your mother threw one leg over the goat's back, facing the rear end. Holding the goat between her legs, she bent over and, with a hand on either side, she began milking. I was laughing at the sight, when all of a sudden the goat began to stir. I can't say for sure how it happened, but the rope came loose and your mother did not have time to jump off.

"This unlikely pair took off across the lawn with McTavish dancing about behind them, which only made the goat run faster. Your mother's surprised look will always be with me, her feet pedaling furiously, trying to keep her balance!" Nan was laughing so hard the water hose fell from her hands. Emma reached for it.

"It all ended in the lilac bushes. There was Madeleine under the goat, who was now trying to butt her farther into the bushes. I was running towards them, and by now my laughter had turned to fear. As the goat backed up for a better run at your mother, McTavish appeared from out of nowhere, growling and nipping at the goat's heels.

"Just as I got there, the goat wheeled about and went for the little dog. He was tossed about six feet into the air, landed, and came back for more. He dodged and rushed at the old nanny goat, but again he was thrown. This time he lay there, limp and silent. Just then, Grandpa Douglas came to our rescue, and got hold of the goat. Madeleine and I picked up poor McTavish, who was limp and unconscious, and rushed him into the house. She kept repeating, 'McTavish saved my life! He saved my life! Oh, the brave little fellow!'

"The local vet came over right away. By then, McTavish was tucked between the white sheets of Madeleine's bed with his head on the pillow! Madeleine was so frightened. She kept stroking his head and pleading with him to get better.  Not long after that, although it seemed like many hours, he was pronounced bruised but healthy by the vet, and a hero by all. From that day on, he was Madeleine's dog."

SUCCESS

Tender-Handed stroke a nettle
And it stings you for your pains;
Grasp it like a man of mettle
And it soft as silk remains."

Fear

TEN

The Lady

Emma looked over to the little crazy quilt floating over the lady-slippers. It was gently swaying back and forth to an unheard beat. Nan paused, and a smile crossed her face as she walked over to the delicate flowers and started the other part of the story.

"Lady came to us from the quarter-horse farms over in High River. John Parsons was so fond of your mother, and she was always out there helping with the horses. When she turned twelve, he gave Lady to her as a birthday gift. It turned out to be the gift of a lifetime. From the day she arrived till the day she died, she was a lady. She had the kindest eyes, always filled with trust and love. Madeleine lived in the stable for weeks when Lady first arrived. They were inseparable. McTavish was wonderful with the mare: he took to sleeping in the paddock with her, for which I was very grateful, since he had always been sneaking up to sleep with Madeleine and leaving paw marks on the bedding.

"It was good for your mother to have the mare; it gave her a sense of responsibility and pride. When Lady came of age, we hired a trainer and every day Madeleine would ride, with McTavish following close behind. The mare and your mother grew up together. It wasn't long before they were competing in horse shows. More valuable than that was the time they spent together. There was an incredible bond between them, beautiful to observe.

"The whole town got used to seeing the inseparable trio. They'd go off for hours into the countryside. A ride I took with them one afternoon, long ago, remains a special memory. We were walking our horses on the path, and Madeleine asked if it would be all right to canter ahead. I stopped to watch them. It was as if your mother had become part of the mare. Lady always appeared to be on springs, like a deer. She galloped effortlessly into the valley, Madeleine sitting so naturally and free, her long black hair streaming back. McTavish was right behind them, a black and white shadow. It was like a dream, a flashback to another era. I realized then that your mother was a very special daughter. Lady helped me to realize that." Nan paused and reached out for Emma. "Lady really helped your mother through those difficult years. Her quiet, lady-like dignity seemed to rub off on your mother."

"McTavish was the busiest little dog in town. Although he preferred to be with the mare, he'd go to the school to meet Madeleine. Next, he would check on Alexandra and Jason, and then be off to run alongside Lady as the trainer put her through her paces. After eating with us, and taking a walk with Grandpa Douglas, he'd go down to the stable to sleep with Lady.

It was something to see: he'd sleep curled up right beside her.

"Madeleine and Lady had been in a lot of horse shows, and they were doing so well. By now, Lady was five years old and Madeleine was sixteen. It looked like they would go to the Nationals in the late fall. I was so proud of them both, and I almost envied the bond between them.

"One night we were awakened by barking from the back garden. Grandpa went down, and there was McTavish, frantically racing about. When he saw Douglas, he ran for the stable. Lady was very sick. The vet came out right away and told us it was severe colic. For no reason, since her food and routine were the same — but she was down and very ill.

"Madeleine was beside herself with worry and tears. Grandpa Douglas and I felt so helpless. Right away we took her out to the veterinary clinic and, after looking into our daughter's eyes, we said, 'Spare no expense, just save the mare!'

"The vets worked through the night, but to to no avail. When Doctor Anderson came to tell us, he had tears in his eyes. 'We just can't save her; you've got to let her go.' We were in a state of complete shock. It just couldn't be possible!

"I took Madeleine in to see the mare for the last time. McTavish was with us. When we approached the enclosure, Lady lifted her head and nickered. McTavish rushed over to her, franti- cally licking her face. Madeleine walked in and put her arms around the mare's neck. Lady's huge brown eyes were filled with pain, and her head rested on Madeleine's shoulder. I couldn't watch any more and, as I walked away, I looked over to see Doc Anderson, silently crying as he leaned up against the barn door. There was a feeling of despair and helplessness in us all.

"Madeleine proved to be stronger — and braver — than any of us; she ended up consoling everyone. Lady was buried out at the Parsons Ranch and we put up a marker for her. It reads, 'Here Lies a True Lady.'

"From that day on, McTavish would not eat; he just moped about in the horse stable. Most of the time, he curled up in a corner of Lady's box stall. Madeleine became very withdrawn and refused to come out of her room. It was a terrible time. But Mr. Parsons came through for us all. About two weeks later, he drove up with a horse trailer and called for Madeleine. 'I have something for you, young lady, and I really need your help.' He opened the trailer door, and there stood a brindled colt. He was quite young, about four months. 'His mother has died, and I just don't have the time to care for him. Can you please help me, Madeleine?'

"Madeleine, who had been standing dejectedly off to the side, peered into the trailer. Just then, the little colt whinnied. 'Well, I guess I could...,' she replied, and walked into the trailer.

"Together, they escorted the long-legged colt to the stable. McTavish was in the corner of Lady's box stall; he barely raised his head when they entered. The young colt walked hesitantly over to the dog. Nose to nose, they examined each other. McTavish gave a few tentative sniffs, then slowly walked back to the corner of the stall. The colt followed, but McTavish ignored him. The next morning, they were asleep together. I guess the colt just persisted, and finally won the dog's heart."

"What was the horse's name, Nana Em?"

"Why, it was Dusty —your lovely horse, Dusty!"

Emma smiled up at her grandmother. "Oh, Nan, he really is a beauty, isn't he?"

"Yes, and he healed a lot of broken hearts. Of course, we never forgot our beloved Lady, but Dusty won over your mother's heart, and they spent wonderful years together."

"Look! Here comes McTavish now!"

A small black and white collie trotted down the path and greeted them both with a grin and a wagging tail. The crazy quilt swooped over the little dog. "Isn't he lovely? Can I pet him, please?" The little dog walked up to Emma.

"Look at the quilt, Emma." Nan pointed to the center. "Can you see the fabric photo of McTavish and Lady with your mother?"

Emma peered at the faded fabric and smiled at the young girl in the photo. "Why, Nan, she looks like your father's family, like the Gypsy princess!"

"Yes, that is your mother, with a crimson show ribbon and a big smile!"

Embroidered under the photo were the words "Lady and Madeleine — Loving Friends."

"Where is Lady, Nan? Can we go see her?"

"No, I'm afraid she isn't here right now. There was a young girl, in great need of a true friend and companion. Lady's returned to earth to live again. She is doing wonders for the little girl, and this time she's been promised a long life. Isn't it wonderful?"

Nan reached for Emma's hand, and turned to close the spigot. McTavish walked close to them, and the little crazy quilt pranced ahead to the musical beat of silent hooves.

ELEVEN

The Return

he garden tour was almost over, with Nan and Emma now back to the front porch. Both were well satisfied that the garden was in good order, not one weed missed their scrutiny, every plant was well watered and content.

"Well, my dear, we just have enough time for milk and cookies before you have to leave."

Emma was amazed. "But, Nan, this is Saturday. I don't have school today!"

"I know, dear, but soon you'll have to walk down the rainbow bridge and into your bed."

Emma looked puzzled. She had completely

forgotten the rainbow bridge! Everything in Nan's magic garden seemed so real. She looked questioningly into her grandmother's kind eyes.

At that moment, the sparkling little crazy quilt floated up the steps and onto the verandah, reminding Emma that quilts are not supposed to fly. Tears welled up in her eyes and a huge sob choked in her throat.

"Nan, please, please let me stay. I love it here. I'll be so good, and I can help in the garden." Big, salty tears streamed down her cheeks. "I'll be ever so quiet; you'll never know I'm here!"

Nana Em reached over for the little girl. "I wish with all my heart that you could stay. You know how much I love you, but it is not your time to be here. Please try to understand, Emma, and know that you must go back."

Holding out her arm, she gestured towards the circular wrought-iron table and chairs. "Come over here and let's sit down." Emma followed her, clinging to her grandmother's arm.

"Now, my dear, you must listen very closely to me." She pulled back the big scroll-work chair and Emma sat down. "Emma, you come from a family of traditions and dreams. I want you to carry on and to live your life to the fullest. I want you to experience all the ups and downs of living, to learn the lessons life holds for you."

The little girl sat quietly in the big chair, head bowed, hands clasped tightly in her lap. Her long legs swung nervously back and forth. "But, Nan, I don't want to leave you. I'll miss you too much."

"What would your mother say if you left her now? She is so sad and lonely because of my departure. It would break her heart to lose you, too. Your father would cry, and the cottage would never be the same without you. They will soon move to my house on Walnut Street, and I'm counting on you to care for my garden." The little girl looked up at her grandmother.

"Think of the others, Emma. Your Uncle Jason looks forward to his visits home because of you. You're the one he counts on for script rehearsals and play practice. Whom would he have to entertain on his trips back home? Aunt Alexandra and her family would yearn for you. You'd miss out on so many experiences. You must go on with your life, Emma."

Nan reached out and cupped her granddaughter's chin in her hand. "We have been so fortunate to have this special time together. It doesn't happen to just anybody! I was concerned about you, Emma, and I wanted you to see me here in my special garden.

"I'm happy, dear, and there are so many loved ones here to keep me company. But if you remain sad and withdrawn, I'll never be at ease." Nan bent closer to Emma. "I'll always be with you, right in your heart. From up here I can watch over you, and I'll never leave you."

Emma sighed and looked deep into her grandmother's eyes. "I'll try, Nana, I really will; I won't let you down."

"Thank you, darling. I feel better already. Remember to take good care of my little quilt. One day you'll pass it along to your children, and you'll have to pass on all the history of the fabric pieces."

"I will, Nan, I will."

"Now, let's have a celebration. You are old enough for a tea party, and I want to share it with you."

Nan clapped her hands and the crazy quilt swooped and twirled over the wrought-iron table. She clapped once more and it settled on the table, a sparkling, vibrant tablecloth.

The smiling Nan clapped her hands twice again, and a glowing silver tray and tea service appeared from out of nowhere. Emma's eyes blinked at the sight. Never in her life had she been served from the family silver tea set. It was a wedding gift for Nan and

Grandpa Douglas: Aunt Lydia had shipped it all the way from Scotland. Ever since Emma could remember, it sat all shiny and glistening on the mahogany sideboard in Nan's dining room. It was reserved for ceremonies like christenings, weddings, graduations, and holiday feasts. The silver tray groaned under two platters of cookies, a milk jug, two china cups and saucers, two plates, a silver sugar bowl and teapot, and two lace-edged napkins.

Nan looked over to her granddaughter. "Now, my dear, let's celebrate our special time together!" She poured a small amount of tea into a floral cup and added a generous amount of milk. Holding the cup and saucer towards Emma, she asked, "One sugar or two, my dear?"

Emma smiled and replied, "Two, please, Nana. yes, two would be nice." She reached for the cup and saucer and balanced it on her lap. Nan prepared her own cup of tea with the usual flourish and placed a china plate and napkin in front of Emma. "A cookie, my dear?," she asked as she held out the two trays.

Emma reached and politely took the nearest cookie. Her grandmother looked inquisitively at her. "You have a long journey; perhaps another would do?" Emma reached for a large chocolate walnut brownie.

It was a peaceful sight. McTavish sat close to Emma, begging for cookie crumbs. Teddy was circled about Nana Em's feet, enjoying the warmth of the afternoon. The garden buzzed with the lazy drone of honeybees and insects. It was a memory Emma would treasure for life.

Two cups of milky tea and four cookies later, it was time to leave. Nan set the empty cups and plates on the tray and clapped her hands. The family silver service disappeared in a sparkling white light. Her eyes twinkled. "One of the many advantages of my new home is that I never have to do the dishes!" She chuckled and clapped again, making the crazy quilt float up and off the circular table.

"Emma, my special little quilt will make sure you get home safe and sound. Always remember that it holds love and memories for us all. Whenever you look at it, you will remember our happy times together."

They walked hand in hand down the verandah steps and along the sidewalk. Nan paused at the front gate. "This is as far as I can go, Emma." She drew her granddaughter close to her. "I love you, Emma; remember that I'm always with you. You will never be alone." Tears shone in her eyes, but a warm smile crossed her face. "I'll watch you grow up and I'll share your many adventures. We all will." She hugged the little girl close and kissed her. "Now, off you go! My quilt will help you along the rainbow bridge."

She was interrupted by a bark and shrill whining. McTavish stood close to the little girl, looking up into Nan's eyes. "Why, look who wants to go with you, Emma! I do believe McTavish wants to follow you." The little dog leaned against Emma's leg and smiled up into her face. Nan shook her head and smiled. "Oh, McTavish, Wee Doggie, you are such a rascal. I'll miss you." The dog barked again as if in answer. "Well, off you go, then; I'll have to let you go."

Emma squeezed against her grandmother, enjoying the familiar lavender fragrance and soft embrace. "I'll never forget you, Nana Em...never ever, ever! I love you." Emma smiled up at her grandmother. "It was a magic time, wasn't it?"

She turned abruptly and opened the front gate. McTavish darted ahead of her and the little quilt hovered above her head, slightly in front. She stepped onto the rainbow bridge. McTavish trotted ahead, stopping every few steps to look back to the little girl.

As Emma turned to wave goodbye to Nana Em, she was overcome by the brilliant light flooding the verandah. They were all there, waving in unison: Grandpa Douglas stood with his arm about Nan; Aunt Lydia and Sasha were standing on the verandah; Claude stood off to the side, bowing low; a beautiful couple in tweed jacket and rose-colored gown waved from the steps; a young soldier snapped a salute and a smile at the amazed little girl; Teddy marched along the picket fence with a little garden fairy swooping about his head. Emma stood there mesmerized by the sight.

A sharp, commanding bark from McTavish forced her to turn around and continue down the rainbow bridge.

As Emma approached her room, she could see herself sleeping peacefully beneath the colorful quilt. The warm glow of sleepiness began to stir, and Emma was suddenly happy to be so close to her feather bed. The crazy quilt hovered above the sleeping Emma and suddenly merged with the quilt draped over the little girl. Emma felt a warm tingling sensation and a rush as she crawled into the bed. The dream-time Emma had returned.

McTavish jumped up on the bed and snuggled close to Emma. She stirred and woke just long enough to receive a wet, sloppy kiss from the little dog. It felt good to be back.

The dappled sunlight danced across the crazy quilt and the sleeping Emma. She began to stir, and soon the morning sun was too bright to ignore.

Emma opened her eyes and reached out for McTavish. He was nowhere to be seen! Alarmed, she sat up in bed and called his name. A knock at the bedroom door interrupted her, and in walked Emma's mother.

"Good morning, darling. How was your night under Nana's quilt?"

The little girl drew her knees up and leaned forward. "Mama, you'll never believe what I did last night! I visited Nan in her garden. Nothing has changed. It's a magic place. She doesn't have to do the dishes. Everything blooms all year long. I saw fairies, and I saw McTavish...."

Her mother sat on the side of the bed. "Sh-h-h, dear, you're rambling on. What do you mean, you saw McTavish?"

"Really, Mama! He came with me down the rainbow bridge; he was just here!" Emma reached for her mother and held her close. "I know all about Lady and about John Penn!"

Her mother drew back and looked deep into Emma's eyes. She didn't question the little girl at all; she just knew it was true. "How is Nan, Emma? Is she happy?"

"Oh, yes, Mama, she's with us all the time, and we don't have to be sad any more." The bedroom door swung open and Emma's father appeared. He was holding a small, furry, black and white bundle.

"Good morning, Princess. Look what we have for you!" He walked over to the side of the bed. The little bundle suddenly wiggled loose and sprawled onto the bed. Emma squealed with delight at the sight. It was a border collie pup!

Two black button eyes, a cold, wet nose and pink tongue soon made contact with the little girl. Emma held up the wriggling puppy and smiled. Looking deep into his eyes, she knew that McTavish was with her.

"What do you want to name him, Emma?," her mother asked.

"We'll call him McTavish, after your dog, Mama. Would that be all right with you?"

Emma's mother hesitated, as if to ask something else. But, looking at the smiling little girl and the puppy, she shrugged her shoulders instead. "Of course it's all right."

"He certainly is the spitting image of McTavish," Madeleine thought to herself. "Whatever happened last night, I am grateful to have my child back to normal. Thanks, Mum."

Emma looked about her room. Yes, it was good to be back. Her parents stood by the bed, enjoying the scene. Emma looked up at them both. "Let's choose a special place for

Nana's quilt today, somewhere we can all enjoy it."

"How about the stairwell, Emma? That way, we'll pass it each day. I'll go measure to be sure it will fit." Emma's mother started for the door.

Her father said, "I'll make a special frame for it. I know Nana would like that." As he turned to leave, Emma yawned and stretched her arms high above her head. Yes, it was good to be home!

From the corner of her eye, Emma could see the left corner of the bright little quilt. It seemed to be fluttering ever so slightly. Her eyes grew wide as it began to rise. Out from the fringed edge appeared two black eyes and a wet nose. Emma laughed at the sight. It was McTavish, Wee Doggie!

She leaped out of bed and gathered the quilt and the puppy into her arms. Cradling them both, she started out of her room. Then she paused; slowly turning, she whispered, "Thank you, Nana Em. I love you."

*Thanks to my grandmothers
Adeline Shantz & Bessie Baker,*

To Grandad Jim Baker,

Grandpa Baca, & Grandpa Bigland,

To Aunt Ora Harlan,

To Auntie Muriel & Uncle Harry Hays,

To Uncles Chris Bigland & Jake Evans,

And to Professor Bill Johnson

— the special threads in my cloth of life.

Afterword

Everyone has a special relative who leaves warm, endearing memories. Perhaps it is a grandmother, a grandfather, or maybe an eccentric aunt or cousin who adds glitter and color to our heritage. I have been truly blessed with a great mixture of characters in my background. Thanks to them, my life has never been dull; from these relatives, I've inherited a strong sense of tradition.

My grandmother Adeline Shantz loved to garden, and people would come from miles around just to see her flowers. Her secret for such a profusion of blooms was an elixir blended from horse manure and rainwater. A gunny sack of this special blend would be immersed in the huge wooden rain barrel for several days. We were severely chastised if we came from the ranch without a sack of the precious substance. She was the only grandmother I knew who preferred horse manure to cologne and candies.

She was incredibly independent, having lost her husband to pneumonia early in their marriage, and having raised three children alone through the Depression. Shantzie worked at many jobs — cleaning lady, grocery clerk, piano player — never losing her dignity or sense of humor. She sang in her church choir and loved to tell risqué jokes. Four days before her death, she was up on the roof clearing the snow: always the independent one. When she died, the priest broke down during the service because he had lost a dear friend. On her gravestone are the words "Your Garden is My Memory."

Grandma Baker was from Stillwater, Oklahoma; she immigrated to Canada with my grandfather in the 1920's. She endured a great deal. Asthma was her heaviest cross to bear. I can remember, as a little girl, noticing that her arms were black and blue from the needle marks, but she would brush away my questions and entertain me with stories about her childhood. Grandma Baker was a real lady, one who always dressed properly and was gracious to all. She read her Bible every day, and always had her needlework nearby. Grandma Baker died when I was only ten years old, but I can still remember her smell: Chanel #5 and baby powder. I loved to be hugged by her. Her skin was so soft and cool, and her bosom was large and comforting.

Uncle Jake was married to Grandma Baker's sister Blanche, a beautiful woman with a flair for the exotic. Depending on which relative you asked, she was a spoiled brat or a wonderful, gorgeous woman. Uncle Jake adored his eccentric wife. He was a sergeant in the American army for the sole purpose of gambling. Besides money, Aunt Blanche was the recipient of jewelry, cars, and fur coats, thanks to his expertise at poker. They never had children of their own but doted on their nieces and nephews.

My favorite memory of Uncle Jake is from my early years, when he would play dolls with me. That is, he would be the baby and I'd put him to sleep on the sofa and cover him up with a quilt! He was a very obliging baby, with a cigar, who slept peacefully for the few hours I spent playing. No one could disturb him, because he was my baby doll. A great way to get out of the daily chores!

Aunt Muriel and Uncle Harry, my godparents, raised me from the time I was fourteen. I was loved unconditionally by them both. Aunt Muriel has Alzheimer's. It is a slow, insidious disease that robs its victims of memories and dignity. As their son Dan says, "We've lost her, Judie. You have to face it: the mother we've known is gone." I find it hard to accept, for not only am I losing a beloved mother, I am losing my one stronghold of tradition.

It was Aunt Muriel who taught me how to drink tea from a china cup and which fork went with each course. I felt safe and secure with her strict rules of conduct. She taught me to be comfortable with people from all walks of life, to take pride in my intelligence and background. She was always there for me with words of encouragement and praise.

It was painful to go home this time, because I can feel it all slipping away. The house is exactly as it was years ago. The silver service gleams on the dining-room sideboard. My bedroom hasn't changed in all the years I've known her. At the foot of my bed is a satin comforter: one side is pale pink and the other side is green. It is folded so that I can reach down and pull it up over me without getting out of bed. The cool satin feels good against my face. Sometimes, when I sleep under this comforter, I can forget that she will leave us, and I believe everything is all right.

We lost Uncle Harry several years ago. He was a most amazing man and better educated than some Ph.D.'s. Completely self-taught, he was one of those rare people who truly enjoy learning — always reading, always questioning. To others he was the Mayor of Calgary, a successful cattleman, Minister of Agriculture, and Senator Hays. To me he was simply "my Uncle Harry." In all the years I lived with him, he never raised his voice or talked down to me.

Uncle Harry kept a jar of quarters in the top drawer of his dresser. One day I went to their bedroom and took three dollars in quarters. I left an I.O.U. scrawled on a piece of foolscap in the jar. And that wasn't the only time. When I could, I would pay it back: he would mark off the debt in red ink. In all those years we never spoke about it: it was our little secret. Today, I still owe him eleven dollars and fifty cents!

I was not a dedicated student in high school, far more interested in horses, boys, and social outings. Whenever I brought home a poor report card, he would gently say, "I hated school; in fact, I only made it to grade eight, and I was expelled at least a dozen times. Now, you are very intelligent, Judie; I know you can do better. Let's see what you do next time." Of course, I would work twice as hard because Uncle Harry believed in me. He was clever like a fox!

Aunt Muriel made sure I had piano lessons. After a few months, I could play several ragtime pieces; my